Everyone says I'm little.
I really don't agree.
If only they could see what I see
When I look at me.

There's no such thing as...

by LeUyen Pham

Alfred A. Knopf 🐎 New York

A little light?

No, a
welcoming
light.

A little snowflake?

No, a **unique snowflake.**

A little fish?

No, a
brave fish.

A little idea?

No, a
fantastic
idea.

FLAVOR:
BLUEBERRY
TOFFEE
BERRY
LEMON
MINT
VANILLA
CHOCOLATE
STRAWBERRY

WORLD'S GREATEST
ICE CREAM
MACHINE

A little letter?

I doubted if I should eve

I shall be telling this with a

somewhere ages and ages hen

Two roads diverged in a wood,

I took the one less traveled by,

And that has made all the differe

Puck: If we shadows have offended,
Think but this, and all is mended,
That you have but slumber'd here
While these visions did appear,

"I'm afraid I can't put it more clearly," Alice replied,
very politely, "for I can't understand it myself, to
begin with; and being so many different sizes in a
day is very confusing."
"It isn't," said the Caterpillar.
perhap you haven't found it so yet," said
ave to turn into a chrysa-
after

you drink my medicine?
e did not a er. Already she was reeling in the air.
t is the ma with you? cried Peter, suddenly afrai
as poisoned er," she told him softly," and now I am going
to ad."
"O Tink, did you drink it to save me?"
"Why, Tink, how dare you drink my medicine?"
"Yes."
"But why, Tink?"
Her wings would scarcely carry her now, but in reply she alighted
on his shoulder and gave his nose a loving bite. She whispered in his ear
"You silly cow", and then, tottering to her chamber, lay down on the bed.
His head almost filled the fourth wall of her little room as he knelt
near her in distress. Every moment her light was growing fainter; and he

No, an
important
letter.

" said the Lion thoughtfully, "if I had
I should not be a coward."

ou brains?" asked the Scarecrow,

ose so. I've never looked to see," replied the Lion,

oing to the 'Great Oz to ask him to give me some,"

d the Scarecrow, "for my head is stuffed with straw."

am going to ask him to give me a heart," said the
an.

am going to ask him to send me back to

," added Dorothy.

you think O d give m

et them run over it.
could not make out wh
was saying that she the
believed in fairies
here were no child
essed all who
fore near

u believe
nk sat up in be
She fancied she hear
again she wasn't sure.
"What do you think?" he shouted
"If you believe," he
don't let Tink die."

Simple Simon met a pieman
Going to the fair.
Said Simple Simon to the pieman
"Let me taste your ware."
Said the pieman to Simple Simon
"Show me first your penny."
Said Simple Simon to the pieman
"Indeed I have not any."
Simple Simon went a-fishing
For to catch a whale.
All the water he had got
Was in his mother's pail.

d bending down beside the glowi
urmur, a little sadly, how Love fle
nd paced upon the mountains ove
And hid his face amid a crowd of

The sixth sick sheik's
sixth sheep's sick.

A little hand?

No, a
strong
hand.

A little line?

No, an
inspiring line.

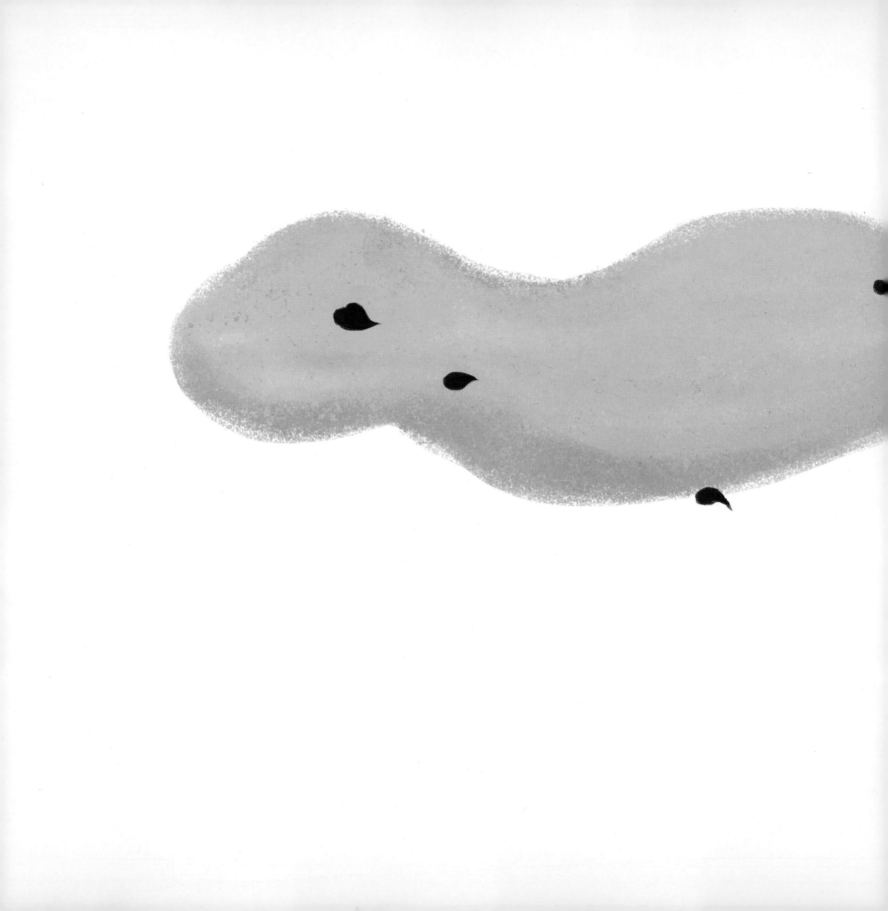

A little gift?

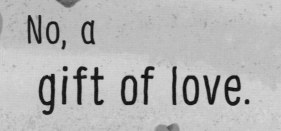

No, a
gift of love.

Little?

Amazing, wonderful, incredible ME.

THIS IS A BORZOI BOOK PUBLISHED BY ALFRED A. KNOPF

Copyright © 2015 by LeUyen Pham

Library of Congress Cataloging-in-Publication Data
Pham, LeUyen, author, illustrator.
There's no such thing as little / by LeUyen Pham.   Pages   cm.
Summary: Reveals how things that seem little are actually very important, such as a little light that is really a welcoming light, or a little idea that is actually a fantastic idea.   ISBN 978-0-385-39150-4 (trade) — ISBN 978-0-385-39151-1 (lib. bdg.) — ISBN 978-0-385-39152-8 (ebook)   [1. Values—Fiction. 2. Perception—Fiction.] I. Title. II. Title: There is no such thing as little.   PZ7.P4486 The 2015   [E]—dc23   2014009037

The text of this book is set in 30-point Supernett cn Regular.

MANUFACTURED IN CHINA
April 2015
10 9 8 7 6 5 4 3 2 1
First Edition

For Amazing Adrien,
Cool Chlöe,
and Super Sébastien

Artwork on pages 36—37 is an homage to the following artists or works of art (clockwise, from top left):

AUGUSTE RODIN. Sketch inspired by the statue *Young Mother in the Grotto*, 1885. 36 x 28.2 x 24 cm. Musée Rodin, Paris, France. **GEORGES SEURAT.** *A Sunday Afternoon on the Island of La Grande Jatte*, 1884. 207.5 x 308.1 cm. Art Institute of Chicago. **EDGAR DEGAS.** *Dancer Adjusting Her Slipper*, 1873. 33 x 24.4 cm. Metropolitan Museum of Art, New York. Inspired by the works of **PABLO PICASSO** (1881–1973). **JEAN-AUGUSTE-DOMINIQUE INGRES.** *La Grande Odalisque*, 1814. 91 x 162 cm. Musée du Louvre, Paris, France. **GEORGES DE LA TOUR.** *Magdalen with the Smoking Flame*, 1640. 128 x 94 cm. Musée du Louvre, Paris, France. **PIERRE BONNARD.** *The Checkered Blouse*, 1892. 61 x 33 cm. Musée d'Orsay, Paris, France. **CLAUDE MONET.** *Woman with a Parasol*, 1875. 100 x 81 cm. National Gallery of Art, Washington, D.C. Inspired by the works of **CY TWOMBLY** (1928—2011).